Powerful Performance Appraisals

How to Set Expectations and Work Together to Improve Performance

Powerful Performance Appraisals

How to Set Expectations and Work Together to Improve Performance

By
Karen McKirchy

CAREER PRESS
3 Tice Road
P.O. Box 687
Franklin Lakes, NJ 07417
1-800-CAREER-1
201-848-0310 (NJ and outside U.S.)
Fax: 201-848-1727

POWERFUL PERFORMANCE APPRAISALS
Cover design by Barry Littman
Printed in the U.S.A. by Book-mart Press

To order this title, please call toll-free 1-800-CAREER-1 (NJ and Canada: 201-848-0310) to order using VISA or MasterCard, or for further information on books from Career Press.

Library of Congress Cataloging-in-Publication Data

McKirchy, Karen.
    Powerful performance appraisals : How to Set Expectations and work together to improve performance / by Karen McKirchy.
        p.   cm.
    Originally published: How to conduct win-win performance appraisals. National Press Publications, 1994.
    Includes index.
    ISBN 1-56414-367-8 (pbk.)
    1. Employees, Rating of. 2. Performance standards. I. Title.
HF5549.5.R3M285 1998
658.3'125--dc21   98-13954

Contents

Introduction

Whether you are a supervisor, manager, or team leader, you lead people who must grow, and that growth can be managed! It is important to understand that you do not get paid for what *you* do; you get paid for what *your people* do. The performance appraisal provides you with the opportunity to direct your employees' attention to the things that really matter. You're judged on the results you're able to achieve, but these results must be achieved through others.

This book will help you achieve better results by developing an honest, productive relationship with your people. It tells you not only what you should do, but also how you should do it.

An effective appraisal system takes two forms: formal performance appraisals and ongoing performance feedback appraisals. During formal performance appraisals, a specific time is set aside to meet with the employee and a formal record of this meeting becomes part of the employee's permanent personnel record. Ongoing performance feedback appraisals, on the other hand, are useful for behavior modification and ongoing communication. They set the stage for many of the issues that will be addressed in the formal, sit-down performance appraisal. The techniques we discuss are applicable to both types of appraisals. However, the focus of this book is on the dynamics of the successful formal, sit-down performance appraisal.

You'll learn how to establish a work climate that is conducive to productive performance appraisals, and be able to initiate and maintain positive communications with your employees about their work performance. You'll also learn to set expectations and produce better results.

Chapter 1

How to Create "Same-Side-of-the-Desk" Thinking

Performance appraisal objectives

Performance appraisals involve setting goals, judging the results achieved, and creating performance criteria that can be met and measured over and over again for each of your employees' job descriptions. You should focus on three things:

1. Performance, not personalities.

2. Valid, concrete, relevant issues, rather than subjective emotions and feelings.

3. Reaching agreement on what the employee is going to improve in his performance and what you are going to do.

The Appraisal Cycle

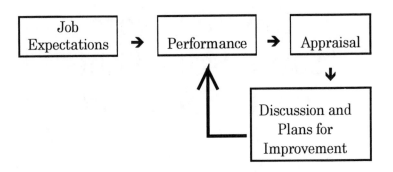

In conducting performance appraisals, you need to make it very clear that *your objective is performance, not personality* issues. This is a big step towards "same-side-of-the-desk" thinking. Together, you and your employee look at what can be done to solve performance problems.

How not to do it

Supervisor: You are always late. Some people in your department think you are lazy.

Employee: I am not lazy. If you think that, you don't understand me at all.

By implying that the employee is lazy, personality issues, emotions, and defenses immediately take over. Saying that the employee is always late isn't quantified. Instead, to make it a factual performance issue, it must be measurable five days out of the last 15, for example.

How to do it

Supervisor: You need to focus on being here on time. Some of your customers call you at 8 a.m., and you're not here to take care of them.

Employee: You are right. I can't get the same level of sales from them as from my other customers. Maybe that's the reason.

Supervisor: Is there anything I can do to help you?

By focusing on specific, often numeric or recorded information, the facts become the facts, rather than feelings. Facts can be addressed. Feelings escalate and become the foundation for self-justification, blame, and continued poor performance.

How not to do it

Supervisor: You are always late. You are never here when your key accounts call.

Employee: I haven't been late that much. [*(Thinking)* You just don't like me, so you are exaggerating.] Get off my back.

How to do it

Supervisor: You have been late 10 of the last 30 days. You're missing key account calls.

Employee: I didn't realize it was that much! I'm always behind with my key accounts. That's probably why.

Supervisor: Is there anything I can do to help you?

Performance appraisal essentials

Be very clear in your communications. Use a 1-2-3 format:

1. Attempt to eliminate any misunderstandings.
2. Quantify specifically *what* is expected from the employee.
3. Describe exactly *when* it is expected.

The attitude you want to take is that you and the employee are partners in successful problem-solving.

How not to do it

Supervisor: This can't continue. If you don't change, there will be serious consequences.

Employee: Okay. I'll do better.

In this episode, you use threats but no measurement; you have expectations with no consequences and specify no time frame when action will be taken.

How to do it

Supervisor: This can't continue. Beginning tomorrow you are expected to be here by 8 a.m. to handle your job. If you are not here, I will give key accounts who call in to another representative. When your key accounts decline by 10 percent, your salary will be adjusted accordingly, and if we reach 20 percent, we will reassign your area to someone else.

> **Employee:** That's pretty harsh. I'm just a little late.
> **Supervisor:** No. You are missing key contact calls because you are a "little" late, as you call it.

These are the basic components of good performance communications. If you are successful in executing the basic components, you gain the following advantages:

- You are forced to assess and realize that an employee's poor performance could be the result of inadequate management. Your attention is focused on what you need to do and say. Once you realize the role you play, the steps you take can focus on the relationship between you and your employee, helping it to function productively on an adult-to-adult level.
- You provide employees with feedback on their performance, enabling them to learn what's expected to become a more successful member of your team.
- You can recognize and reinforce good performance and set goals for the future. When goals are set by the employee, there is more motivation to achieve those goals.
- You are given another tool for helping employees solve problems, one of your most important tools—the tool that gets results !

The performance appraisal process provides useful feedback, helping you and your company optimize human assets. New goals and objectives are agreed upon and work teams can be restructured for maximum efficiency. The development of your department must reflect the interests, abilities, and motivations of the employees who comprise it; otherwise, achieving objectives will be nearly impossible. These goals emerge through the "same-side-of-the-desk" thinking of a well-planned performance system.

The performance appraisal serves as the basis for you and your employee to strengthen your relationship and become a solid team, two adults working toward a common, agreed-upon goal. It forces you to look at your own actions to see what supervision the employee requires for better performance. Your job is to identify quickly the techniques that work with individual employees and adjust your own style to get the maximum productivity from them.

Leadership, your style, and performance improvement

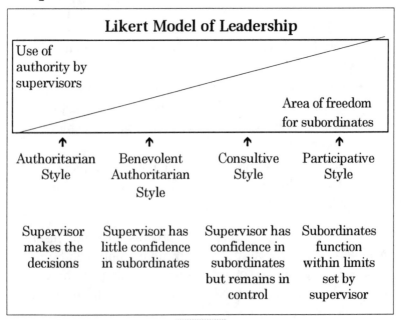

Likert Model of Leadership

Use of authority by supervisors

Area of freedom for subordinates

Authoritarian Style	Benevolent Authoritarian Style	Consultive Style	Participative Style
Supervisor makes the decisions	Supervisor has little confidence in subordinates	Supervisor has confidence in subordinates but remains in control	Subordinates function within limits set by supervisor

Look at each end of this chart, beginning on the left side. Some employees cannot deal with too much independent decision-making. They need a supervisor to decide and direct their work, using an authoritarian style.

Authoritarian

Employee: I don't know how to handle the call to ABC Company. They never respond, and I never get a sale with them. I just don't know what to do.

Supervisor: Handle them as we handled that call with XYZ Company. You offered to come over to see their operation. They liked that, and that opened the door for you. Call them right now.

Employee: You are right. That's what I need to do!

Participative

Supervisor: What problem do you see handling the DEF Company account?

Employee: I can't get them to make a commitment. We're just one of a number of companies calling on them right now. They think our product is a commodity, and they want to buy only on price.

Supervisor: How do you think you should handle it?

Employee: I would like to invite them over for a tour of our facility to show them how advanced we are in quality management. I think we can distinguish ourselves from the competition in that area and show them the value added with our products, that there really is a difference, not only with our products but also with our people.

Supervisor: That's a fine idea. How can I help?

You'll notice that in the last example, the supervisor lets the employee solve his own problem (participative).

In contrast, in the first example (authoritarian), direct commands are given for the employee to execute. The supervisor knows that the employee will execute them well but that he has trouble seeing the right thing to do on his own. Therefore, the supervisor tells the employee in no uncertain terms (authoritarian) what should be done.

Your leadership style must change with different issues and different employees. This is not the same as being wishy-washy or a constantly changing person whom no one can get a fix on. It means that you carefully consider what will work for each individual and situationally apply a technique or a series of techniques to accomplish the objective. This does not mean bearing the entire responsibility for your subordinate's performance yourself. The employee has equal responsibility. But it's your job, as a leader, to see that he has been provided with everything necessary to meet his job responsibilities.

When employees hear performance feedback from a well-done appraisal session, they have real, solid information on which to act. Without such information, they're guessing, and their record usually indicates inadequacies. Time spent guessing is wasted, unproductive time. You can't afford to have your people work in a "guessing" mode, and neither can your company.

How not to do it

Supervisor: So, let's close by focusing on the fact that you need to make more good sales calls each day.

Employee: *(after the meeting)* My supervisor talked about how I needed to make more good calls each day. But what's a "good" call. I guess I'll just make more calls.

Obviously, the company is only interested in the number of calls, not how well they're done or the results. I'll just fill up my call sheet.

You can see in the above example that the supervisor's guidance is incomplete. What really constitutes a "good" sales call? The employee may increase the number of calls, but he is left guessing how to improve the quality or the results.

Positive performance feedback

Sometimes when people think of performance appraisals, they think only of the negative. While it is important to put out the most threatening fires, giving positive feedback to employees is very important. This is especially true when employees have just made a difficult change. They need to know you're watching and recognizing their work and that they're achieving results.

If you do have negative feedback to give, a well-known successful technique, called "insertion," usually proves successful. First, a positive comment is made, then the negative feedback is "inserted," and a positive comment finally closes. The overall effect on the employee is positive, while a negative concern is still being addressed. This technique is especially useful with an employee who is trying hard, making progress, or who just doesn't handle criticism well. It's not recommended where stern warnings are required, however.

How to do it

Supervisor: I really like the way you've taken control of the DEF account. *(Positive)*

Employee: Thank you. It felt good to finally get them as a regular customer.

Supervisor: The TUV account is causing a lot of problems. *(Negative)* We need to discuss what to do about it. You handled the ABC account well. *(Positive)* How can we use what we learned on ABC to solve the problems with TUV?

The performance appraisal process helps determine where an employee is in his development and helps the company better deploy the skills of its employees to achieve the business objectives. Here are a few tips you'll find helpful. *Remember: Real-time feedback motivates!*

- The time to correct an employee's mistake is when it happens. Don't allow an error to become a habit.
- The performance appraisal process should be a summary of the day-to-day realizations the employee and you share.

- The magic isn't in the appraisal form, it's in the people trying to work together to create a better future.
- Properly conducted, the performance appraisal process provides as much relationship improvement as performance improvement.

The pace of business today is hectic and will likely continue as the trend toward downsizing/rightsizing continues and worldwide competitive pressures increase. The time to talk about good and bad performance is when it happens, when the issues are clear and not influenced by the rush of memories.

Employees become motivated when they feel you are there with them, caring, coaching, and understanding the events that occur. You want to stop something before it becomes larger, so by dealing with it quickly you can get it out of the way and move on to other matters, such as increasing productivity. By dealing with things as they happen, you also avoid festering feelings.

The formal, sit-down performance appraisal

If you realize you have failed to change your employee's behavior through daily interaction, you can use the formal, sit-down performance appraisal to finally get your point across.

Properly handled, the formal, sit-down performance appraisal becomes a summary of observations as well as a solid platform for new understanding of how to achieve the best results possible.

Once you observe less-than-optimal results, it's time to revisit your employee's job description. It describes accepted expectations and offers a format for discussing where performance has slipped. The employee can then modify his actions and you can provide appropriate help. An honest discussion of shortfalls and performance results should refocus both you and your employee. The form itself is only a guideline to help the conversation focus productively.

The magic comes when the two people communicate, break through their problems and obstacles, celebrate their success, and plan for more. The employee in this framework feels a part of the process, rather than a victim of it. The relationship between team members also can improve.

Performance improvement often follows naturally because you took time to refocus your employee's personal pride. Employees are normally highly motivated with a desire to please. Use this to your advantage in directing their actions and building your relationship with them.

Salary and performance appraisals

Often the review of an employee's performance is tied to his salary. This system is usually referred to as "pay for performance." When it's time to determine how much of a raise, if any, an employee will receive, the performance appraisal becomes the determining factor. The better the performance, the greater the raise—at least, that's the underlying assumption. On the surface, pay for performance sounds good, but there can be several problems when pay increases depend on the outcome of the appraisal meeting.

First, there is the tendency of the employee to want to discuss examples of stellar performance and to explain away anything that might negatively affect the increase. The meeting can turn into a battle of explanations between manager and employee, rather than an open discussion of performance and how it can be improved.

Another problem is that company budgets or personnel policies often dictate the amount of increase a manager can give an employee or group of employees. A manager may have to face the fact that business conditions or national cost-of-living figures impose a limit on the raises he can give. In such cases, even though an employee's performance may be better than that of the previous year, the amount of the increase may be lower. This can weaken employee morale and, as a result, future performance.

When the issue of salary, and not the employee's performance, becomes the focus of the appraisal meeting, the benefits of the human touch are quickly lost. Even though salary considerations may not be mentioned directly, they're on everyone's mind throughout the discussion.

To diffuse this conflict, many experts now recommend cutting the ties between salary increases and performance appraisals. One way to do this is with two separate discussions—one focused on pay and one focused on performance. This allows the manager and employee to openly discuss performance without the specter of salary looming overhead. Then when it's time to discuss pay raises, both parties have the same focus for the meeting.

If your organization is one that ties performance to pay increases, all is not lost. Pay for performance also has its share of supporters. They argue that, if you measure performance as accurately and objectively as possible, you can and should use it to determine the amount of a pay increase.

The key to making either system work is for managers to demonstrate that they are concerned about their employees' needs, wants, expectations, and goals—in short, to use the human touch. Managers who do are communicating that, although salary is important, in the long run, it's the way you treat your employees on a daily basis that determines their real success.

Chapter 2

Legal Issues

Employment law

Uniform Guidelines on Employee Selection 1978 is the controlling federal law in the area of performance appraisals. Your company's performance appraisal system is central to nearly all personnel processes: hiring, promotion, demotion, transfer, salary, selection for training, etc. This book will not focus on all the legal ramifications; you need to talk to your legal counsel about such matters. Most well-run companies will train you in-depth in these areas because they hold much of the legal liability. However, your performance reviews must be workable, equitable, ongoing, and as objective as possible, because you and your organization are expected to follow and meet all legal requirements. Lack of knowledge or ignorance of the law is no excuse for violations.

Your performance appraisal must have no adverse impact on any of the areas covered by the law, such as employees':

- Race.
- Sex.
- Religion.
- National origin.

- Age.
- Handicapped status.

These are the major areas covered, but they may not describe all the areas protected by law when you read this. Consult your company's training guide or your personnel manager about any questions. You must understand that if a member of any "protected" group is adversely affected, the performance appraisal practice is illegal. All performance appraisal practices must contain *measuring standards*. What does this mean?

Meeting legal requirements

The Equal Employment Opportunity Commission (EEOC) requires that any measurement used to differentiate between employees must be valid and fairly administered. The Americans with Disabilities Act (ADA) suggests that performance appraisals for people with disabilities will not be conducted any differently than those for other employees. That's why it's important for the appraisal to focus on the requirements listed in the employee's job description. Having specific goals also helps ensure that the appraisal does not focus on areas that could be considered discriminatory.

Measurement standards

Measuring standards are valid when you can:

- Prove content validity—A person must be able to perform this task to do her job.

- Prove construct validity—You must show the relationship between rating scores and traits or skills needed on the job.
- Prove criterion-related validity—You must show the relationship between rating scores and measure of job performance.

In other words, in order to be legal, a certain skill must be shown to be a valid, true, and necessary requirement of the job. Discrimination against protected groups is allowable as long as the discriminating variable is legitimately related to the requirements of the work situation. For example, if the next level job on the factory floor demands the ability to lift 75 pounds above waist height, and a wheelchair-bound employee cannot perform this task, it is acceptable not to promote that person to that job.

You must be able to consistently observe the employee performing the assigned tasks. Your rating criteria must be the same for all employees of the same grade/class/group. But be careful: Using numerical scores increases an organization's liability to validate them. Just because something is expressed in numbers does not automatically make it legal.

Another important aspect to consider is the employee's right to privacy. Employees must have complete access to their personnel files, but others should have controlled access. These records must be accurate, relevant, and current. Discuss with your personnel department any questions you have in these areas, but keep in mind that job-relatedness and fairness are the two controlling principles whenever you put something in writing.

Substantial performance, or even average performance, should not be described in such a way that the employee believes her performance is better than it is. You do a great disservice to your employee and your team when you praise less-than-adequate performance. Besides, you flirt with performance collapse. Employees soon lose confidence in you, their trust sags, and respect falls.

Performance must be described *accurately* and must be based on *documentation.* If an employee is terminated for poor performance, but previous reviews were either good or vague, the employee may have grounds for a wrongful discharge lawsuit. All performance appraisal feedback, as well as any other employee communications, must be free of sexual innuendo or sexual harassment.

Warning! Be careful of rating subjective qualities: attitude, cooperation, enthusiasm, initiative. Subjective ratings are difficult for you or your company to defend in court. Quantifiable areas such as deadlines met, calls made, items produced, quota achieved, etc., are much easier to defend and are more productive for you and your employee.

Chapter 3

Clarifying Needs

Employee needs

Everyone has needs in the workplace. Here are the most important needs from your employee's viewpoint.

1. To know how/what he is doing relative to your expectations and the company's goals.

2. To understand the following:
   - The criteria to be used in the performance appraisal.
   - How his performance will be measured (against which standard).
   - Who will do the appraisal.
   - When the appraisal will be done.
   - What feedback he will get.
   - If he can give input to the process and when.

- What assistance the company will provide in improving performance.

- What the rewards are for above-average performance.

3. To be listened to in the following areas:

   - How things are going on the job in general.

   - Any specific problems he is experiencing.

   - What you, as supervisor, can do to make his job less frustrating and him more effective.

   - What the employee thinks he is doing well and suggested areas for improvement.

4. To receive helpful, constructive feedback.

5. To be treated with dignity and respect.

6. To feel that someone cares.

There are several other factors to consider when looking at the relationship between employee performance appraisals and your employee's needs:

1. The employee's desire to be evaluated varies both within each individual and from individual to individual over time. An individual who believes his performance is good is less concerned about the opinions of others regarding performance. An individual who is success-oriented in his performance is more interested in feedback than one who fears failure.

2. The anticipation of being evaluated is threatening. Therefore, hostility is often directed toward performance appraisers. An employee often views an evaluation as an occasion when he lacks control of his fate, and he is frequently apprehensive and anxious. Individuals with low self-esteem are more apt to feel threatened than those with high self-esteem. Negative reactions to criticism often occur if ongoing support is not available from you.

3. The more an individual is able to influence his evaluator, the more likely he is to accept an evaluation as his own evaluation. The relationship between a supervisor and his associates determines whether the latter accept the former's ratings. An expert appraiser's opinions are more likely to be accepted than those of a nonexpert. Your staff is more likely to accept your ratings if they like and respect you, and an individual is more likely to accept evaluations that are similar to those he has received from other appraisers.

Employer needs

Employers have needs, too! Because the employee is an asset of the company, the employer needs to regularly review and direct productively the contributions its employees make toward achieving the company's objectives. As a manager or supervisor, you must focus yourself on the needs of your organization, including:

1. Performance appraisals that help control quality, performance, and output.
2. A system that identifies both individual employee and departmental training needs.
3. Necessary information for manpower and organizational planning.
4. Recommendations that reinforce or suggest modifications to the employee selection process.
5. A performance system that improves employee morale and offers recognition and reward for above-average performance.
6. An opportunity to talk about how to develop particular employees.
7. Time to talk about the job and what needs to be done to improve.
8. A chance to motivate, teach, and coach. This area is often not clearly recognized by either employer or employee.

A mutuality develops when you pay attention to your employee's needs, and a true sense of respect emerges when your own and the organization's needs are shared with the employee.

Chapter 4

Performance Appraisal Systems

4 types of appraisal systems

The following section lists different types of performance appraisal systems and some of the advantages of each. Carefully read the description of each type. You will find ideas you can use, no matter what style your company currently follows. Four different types of appraisal systems are:

1. Self-directed work teams.
2. Peer appraisal systems.
3. Self-rating systems combined with formal performance appraisal.
4. Other performance systems.

Self-directed work teams

Overview: In this model, the performance appraisal is the primary vehicle for communicating business strategy to employees. Each team has a family of critical measures linked to measures of performance that, in turn, constitute the overall business strategy. These measures are revised annually.

Description: Performance measures usually fall into the following groups:

- Quality.
- Financial—cost and revenue considerations.
- Timeliness.
- Productivity/efficiency.

Associated with each measure are three criteria: a long-term goal, short-term goals, and the minimum standards of performance.

Teams usually:

- Identify behaviors that have the greatest impact on performance.
- Measure behavior and create specific feedback on team performance compared to the goal. Employees keep track of their own performance. Weekly and monthly team meetings are held to identify problems and work through solutions.
- Rely on managers who are trained to reinforce desired behavior as it occurs, not just once or twice a year.

Individual employee performance goals center primarily on learning and development. Goals for an individual might be to improve communication or build problem-solving skills. General actions to achieve these goals might be taking on more leadership responsibilities in meetings (communication) or serving on a task force (problem-solving). Specific tactics might include working on different communication or problem-solving techniques.

Personal contribution to the team's goals might include: quality improvement, cost reduction, or improvements in customer service. Team goals clarify the role of the work-group. Workgroups are charged with the responsibility of accomplishing a "family of measures," five to 10 key measures of performance that the team must monitor, control, and improve.

In summary, the self-directed work team performance appraisal system is one type of system used by companies that utilize work teams. This system allows you to conduct short, ongoing, informal reviews, as well as formal quarterly reviews. It provides the freedom to structure the review in light of individual and team needs. It is not just a paperwork exercise, but real, ongoing communication with no once-a-year surprises.

Peer appraisal systems

Overview: Sometimes you may use this technique to gain additional information, especially when using work teams.

Description: The employee is reviewed by her peers. Feedback is collected from team members, compiled by the appraiser, and used in combination with a more traditional appraisal form.

Advantages: A well-rounded view of performance can be gained by combining a variety of perspectives. It also builds peer accountability.

Disadvantages: Veracity and commitment of your employees. Helping them feel good about the process takes time. Here are some guidelines to making a peer evaluation system work:

1. Start small. Don't try to get everyone to appraise everyone. Begin with one or two peer evaluations. Sometimes the employee picks her own peer evaluators.

2. Protect the confidentiality of all peer ratings. Truthfulness and honest feedback increase when peers know their specific insights will not be exposed. Your employee needs to know "how" she is perceived by the team, not necessarily the specifics.

3. When peers know that performance and income potential come from these ratings, it is very tempting to write favorable reviews. No one wants to take food from someone else. It's important that you de-emphasize punishment, emphasize positive criticism, and keep everyone focused on team success.

4. Do not abdicate your managerial responsibilities to the peer review. The peer review offers valuable information that should support and affirm the key points you choose to appraise. If you are out of step with an employee's peer reviews, rethink your perceptions.

Self-rating systems combined with formal performance appraisal

Overview: Self-rating creates a participative approach to the traditional appraisal method. Employees rate their performance and then review it with you. This is the method we will expand upon in the upcoming section, "The employee self-analysis" in Chapter 5. You can change the rating to reflect the true situation if the employee has rated herself too high or too low. Responsibility for the performance appraisal is delegated to the employee. This method treats people like adults. Your role truly becomes one of counselor, teacher, and coach.

Description: Ninety percent of all employees rate themselves at or below what you would! This high percentage makes the method viable. Your role becomes one of praising, encouraging, and being generally positive to the employee. The employee comes away with a better self-image.

If an employee rates herself correctly, your role becomes one of confirmation and reinforcement. This leads naturally into a "Where do we go from here?" attitude, opening up exploration of further development and improvement.

Ten percent of employees will rate themselves higher than the manager does. Half of them believe their performance is that good. This calls for a response from you. These employees usually aren't trying to fight about their rating; they simply have a different perception. The other half are really troubled, however. They have inflated opinions of themselves, and they sometimes argue. These are the employees who are not happy under any performance appraisal system.

Advantages: Self-rating stands up well in court defenses. Fewer cases go to court when the employee participates in her own performance appraisal than when appraisals are completed only by supervisors.

Other performance systems

You'll probably find one of the following to be the basis for your company's performance appraisal form. Each of the major types is briefly reviewed below.

1. *Rating scales:* Behaviorally anchored rating scales are charted. Key issues are targeted and measured. You sample behavior over the long term and do not rely on short-range judgments and impressions. Such scales reveal the complex behaviors that contribute to successful performance.

2. *Forced rank comparisons:* These are based on the selection of one statement from three to five alternatives that the appraiser thinks most accurately describes employee behavior. Each statement is weighted; therefore, employees with higher scores are deemed to be better than employees with lower scores.

3. *Critical incident:* The appraiser records critical incidents and stores them for communication during the appraisal. This method is generally viewed as ineffective because to be effective the feedback should be given at the time the incident occurred.

4. *Free-form essay:* This system usually consists of a description, in the appraiser's words, of the employee's overall performance, including quantity and quality of work, job know-how, and ability to get along with other employees. The appraiser lists both the employee's good points and shortcomings.

Why do some supervisors fail to conduct performance appraisals?

There are many reasons why you may fail to discuss your employees' performance. You may avoid dealing with your employees because the appraisal form is too complicated. A more subtle form of avoidance involves discussing only the positive aspects, never digging into any negative aspects. Why does avoidance occur?

1. Some people fear the possibility of disagreement and confrontation, as well as accumulation of hostility over past events. Once an argument starts, supervisors feel they have to win. So do the employees. Usually, neither wins.

2. Lack of interpersonal and interviewing skills is another common reason for avoiding employee performance reviews. If you do not know the techniques for directing the appraisal interview, you're not likely to look forward to it.

3. The fear of making matters worse by talking about the review.

4. Effective appraisal interviews depend in part on establishing limited, attainable objectives. If your organization's forms are too complex, they take over the process. Hundreds of items on a form do not lend themselves to pursuing a limited number of objectives. They make it difficult to even start!

5. Who else looks at the forms and why? A superior's review can influence what you do. This reality may overshadow real communication and make the process seem phony.

6. The fact that an employee's work is favorable does not automatically ensure a promotion, but employees sometimes think so. This mistaken notion often results in disappointment for the employee. When you cannot deliver a promotion, you may avoid an employee review for fear of losing that employee.

7. When performance and salary reviews are combined, the overriding message becomes dollars. Performance appraisal and salary review are not very compatible, and combining them leads to less effective and often messy encounters. Some people use separate sessions, but the time to do both slips away.

The performance appraisal is your most effective management tool. Many managers fail to view their people as a business resource and, therefore, fail to manage them accordingly. Business decisions are made every day to invest money in fixing up the "old one" rather than buying a "new one." Your staff should be viewed the same way. It may cost $30,000 or more to replace a professional employee but only $15,000 to $20,000 to retrain or modify a current employee's behavior.

A very profitable business decision is made when you learn to focus your energies on performance appraisals, spending time to help with employee performance. You must accept full responsibility for the success or failure of your human resources, the same way you have accepted full responsibility for nonhuman resources (machinery, deadlines, finances, materials, facilities, products, etc.).

Chapter 5

The Performance Interview

An overview

The actual performance interview is not the beginning or the end of anything. It is the middle step in a continuing, repetitive cycle with the content of each discussion changing.

Your first step is to define the job. Don't be content with a job description that is supplied to you. Look at it carefully to see if it truly relates to your department, your company, and your goals *today*! Ask yourself, "What is it I really want my employee to do?" And if there's more than a 10-percent change from what's written in the job description, rewrite it! Better yet, write it with your employee.

Your second step is to communicate the job effectively to the employee, leveling on what is expected. This goes beyond handing your employee written job specs. It goes to the heart of what is expected and, if appropriate, the when and the how.

The third step in the appraisal cycle is keeping a performance log on each employee and updating it frequently.

The performance log contains the date, the event, the action taken, the result, and the follow-up information on each employee. These are primarily incident reports, including progress reports where you evaluate work in progress. Pick a time period each week to update these logs. It is necessary not only to document extraordinary events but also to make summary entries. Stick to the facts in your entries. Personal feelings or opinions will not be helpful to you later.

The actual performance appraisal should not be too extensive; after all, everyone fails periodically. The purpose of the appraisal is not to communicate all your judgments. You must learn to limit yourself, covering what's possible. You control the appraisal. What you want to accomplish determines how you plan and conduct an appraisal.

- Set your objectives.
- Determine what will be talked about.
- Keep the interview on track.

By keeping the interview on track, you get the employee to want to improve his performance. The key to successful appraisals is being able to answer "yes" to each of these questions:

- Does the employee know what is expected?

- Have you developed objectives for the interview based on your desired results?

- Will you control the appraisal interview and not let an appraisal form do it?

- Have you developed a strategy for the appraisal interview?
- Do you have the necessary skills to do what you want to do?

If you cannot answer "yes" to each of these questions, you are not ready to discuss performance with your employee.

The appraisal form

Before you can become proficient in each aspect of conducting a successful performance appraisal, you must understand how your company expects the performance appraisal to be used. After understanding your company's policy, consider the following:

1. Make sure the form serves your needs as well as the needs of the employee you will be rating. Normally, forms cover too much. If the form is too overwhelming, it's not helpful. Further, when a form deals with attitudes and other abstract behavior, how do you get objective measurements? Abstract behavior is not as objective an assessment as "five days late in the last 30-day period"; yet it is often treated as such. How will you keep from having a negative impact on performance when using the form?

2. The performance appraisal form is not your only basis for employee appraisal. Don't fill out the form and send it in without consulting the employee. Don't change the form after discussing it with the employee, either.

3. Everyone should view and use appraisals professionally. Appraisals are personal and privileged information.

4. Appraisal forms should call for objective data on the employee's performance. Performance should be rated as "satisfactory" or "unsatisfactory" with a space for comments. You and the employee should work on the form together. Each of you should review a blank form in preparation for the meeting and then complete the form in the meeting, utilizing joint discussion without preconceptions.

This approach usually results in the most successful appraisals. You are free to conduct a purposeful appraisal interview without the constrictions of the form. If a form is required, use it. But don't let the form limit a meaningful performance discussion with your employee.

Preparing for the performance appraisal

The following points offer you a step-by-step method for analyzing employee behavior. By looking carefully at your employee's performance and writing down specifics to discuss, you will build your own confidence. This results in a more positive experience for both you and the employee.

The basis for this preparation is a review of your performance log. Review each incident report and progress report you filed. Significant problems should not wait for discussion in a formal review. You don't want to approach the formal performance review with negative surprises. This documentation focuses you on actual performance and experience, rather than on personality issues. As a result, you'll be more likely to remain objective.

1. Formulate positive behavior goals for your employee. During performance appraisals, it's easy to come from the negative point of view, i.e., listing the things that are not being done, etc. *It is better to ask for more of something than less of something.* Express yourself in terms of what is needed. Use a positive rather than a negative approach. For example, the statement, "You are always late" needs to be changed to, "You need to be on time." You may think it's a small change, but, taken all together, such statements can send very powerful messages.

How not to do it

You are never on time.

How to do it

You need to be here on time every day.

How not to do it

You're rigid.

How to do it

You need to be more flexible.

How not to do it

You're too fussy.

How to do it

You need to learn to distinguish between what's important and what's not important on the job.

---

2. Identify what's needed to improve the employee's performance. In what ways should he function more effectively? Determine whether addressing the problem is worth your time. If it's unimportant, you waste your time, the employee's time, and the company's resources on an area where the return is not satisfactory. This is not good business.

3. Concentrate on the causes of the problem, not the symptoms. The solution must be related to the problem or it will be ineffective.

   Consult the following list:

   • Identify "nonperformance."

   • Determine if it is worth the time required to change nonperformance to performance.

   • Does the employee know that the performance is not satisfactory?

   • Does the employee clearly understand what he is supposed to do and when?

   • Are there any obstacles that are beyond the employee's control?

- Does the employee know how to do the job?
- Does a negative result exist if the employee does not perform?
- Have you removed rewards for your employee's nonperformance?
- Could the employee do the task if he wanted to?

4. Collect information without making judgments by talking to the employee. Then you can help him discover what to do differently so that the results will change. Remember, you must identify the *behavior* that is causing the problem.

5. Make sure the employee knows there is a problem. Identify both the *specific behavior changes* you want your employee to make and *what the employee would have to do to convince you* the problem has been solved.

How to do it

Supervisor: *(Thinking)* Martha never listens, and she always seems to misunderstand directions. My goal is to have her listen and understand what I ask her to do. The specific things Martha will have to do to convince me she has accomplished this goal are:

- Doing things the way I ask her to do them, unless she checks with me first.
- Asking me for clarification if she does not understand.
- Repeating back to me the instruction, confirming her understanding.

6. Identify success areas. You must know where the employee is performing effectively and provide *specific* examples in each area. This cannot be emphasized enough. It is important to show positive performance examples as well as negative ones.

7. Review background information. It is helpful to know the employee's length of service with the company, the current projects the employee is working on, the date of the employee's last promotion, the employee's educational and experiential background, etc.

In summary, don't sit down with your employee until you have covered each of the above areas using your performance log on that employee, a record of the employee's attendance, the employee's personnel file, the employee's job description, and the job and career objectives drawn up in your last performance appraisal with your employee as reference. Then you are prepared.

Defining job expectations

Earlier we touched on job descriptions and their importance to the appraisal process. In preparing for the appraisal, you must examine the existing job description. What is its focus in the following areas?

- Customer satisfaction.
- Economic health of the company.
- Innovation.
- Quality.

- Productivity.
- Human resources.
- Organizational climate.

List your own job expectations. Decide what you really expect this person to do on the job in the areas of:

- Objectives.
- Projects.
- Authority.
- Priority.
- Scheduling.
- Results/standards of performance.

What things do *you* value the most?

Appraise performance, not expectations. What are the employee's major strengths and weaknesses? What personal characteristics or habits block greater achievement? What's ahead for this person? Why?

Thought must be given at this point to how each of the above areas will be addressed in the appraisal interview with the employee. If each area is addressed, will it be too much for the employee to handle in one sitting? Which areas are the most important and how will they be covered?

Be conscious of the following tendencies and try to avoid them as you prepare to assess your employee:

- *Trait assessment:* Too much attention to certain characteristics that have nothing to do with the job or are difficult to measure blind us to more important traits.

- *Overemphasis:* Too much emphasis on favorable or unfavorable performance of one or two tasks could lead to an unbalanced evaluation of the overall employee contribution.

- *Bias/prejudice:* Things that have nothing to do with performance, such as race, religion, education, family background, age, handicapped status, and/or sex, do not belong in the evaluation.

- *False reliance:* Relying on impressions rather than the facts is unfair.

- *Misplaced accountability:* Holding the employee responsible for factors beyond his control is unrealistic.

Concentrate on performance measured against mutually understood expectations.

Asking the employee to meet: the personal touch

Your primary objective is to prepare the employee for a meaningful discussion with you. Don't have your secretary or another associate carry the invitation, and don't send a memo. When you ask personally, you have control over the entire process. You don't have to worry about another layer complicating communications. The personal touch is an important component you want to capitalize on at this point, and you want to begin the entire interaction on a positive, personal note.

- Don't combine the meeting with the invitation. Give the employee time to organize his thoughts so his feedback is more helpful to the process. Without sufficient time to prepare, people are normally reactionary and can become resentful.
- Don't underinform or overinform your employee of the details needed for a successful meeting.
- Don't be ambiguous; be clear. Ambiguity can result in anxiety. Anxiety can be counterproductive to good communication.
- Don't say too much or get dragged into answering questions that should be part of the appraisal interview.
- Don't mock the process by making jokes. You'll lose your credibility and any hope of achieving worthwhile objectives.
- Don't arrange the meeting when you are upset or angry.

The best way to ask an employee to meet is to approach him privately. Explain the purpose of the meeting and how you would like him to prepare. This is very important. Suggest that the employee prepare for the meeting by thinking of things he is doing well and areas that need improvement. The employee should also be asked to come prepared to discuss:

1. Job performance issues since the last review.
2. Personal career objectives.
3. Problems or concerns about the present job.
4. Goals for improving performance and productivity.

Finally, ask the employee to think about things you can do to make things better. This sends an important message that you want to hear the employee's input. It shows that you think of the appraisal as a two-way street, that you and the employee are a team. You might want to photocopy the list on page 53 as a tool your employee can use to prepare for his appraisal meeting.

How to do it

Supervisor: *(To employee when no one is near)* I'd like to arrange a time to meet with you to review your work performance. Everyone in the office will be scheduled soon.

Employee: Okay...

Supervisor: I'm going to prepare for this meeting by writing down some of the things you have been doing really well and some of the areas where you can improve. I'd like you to prepare for the meeting by doing the same. First think about the things you are doing well. Then, concentrate on the areas where you feel you could improve.

Employee: I can do that.

Supervisor: Also, I'd like you to think about areas where I could help make your job less frustrating and more satisfying for you. Okay?

Employee: Really? I'll work on it.

Supervisor: Good. How's next Monday at 10 a.m. in my office?

Employee: That will be just fine.

Supervisor: Good. I'll see you then.

Questions the employee can ask as he prepares for his performance appraisal:

- What critical abilities does my job require?
- What were my special accomplishments during this appraisal period?
- What do I like about my job? What don't I like?
- What goals or standards didn't I meet?
- How could my supervisor help me?
- Is there anything that the organization or my supervisor is doing that is hindering my progress?
- How can I become more productive?
- Do I need more experience or training on my current job?
- What have I done since my last appraisal to prepare myself for more responsibility?
- What new goals or standards should be applied for the next appraisal period? Which old ones should be discarded?

Get organized and rehearse each step if you feel it's necessary in order to set the stage for the positive appraisal to follow.

The employee self-analysis

A well-done performance appraisal requires the collaboration of you and your employee. The first step is to understand why the employee's self-analysis is important.

Employees will appreciate your interest in their analysis because it's an expression of interest in them. By listening to your employee's view of his performance, you'll see things from another perspective. The self-analysis involves the employee in the process and helps cement a strong relationship between you. You'll get a much clearer picture of any differences in viewpoint, and you'll get valuable new information on strengths and areas needing improvement.

Communicate to your employee that the purpose is to:

- List areas of major responsibility and accountability.
- Identify areas where the employee thinks he is performing effectively.
- Identify areas for improvement and some specific things he could do to show improvement in each area.
- Help your employee chart realistic goals for the future.

Let the employee know you will also be going through these steps and that you will be comparing notes.

How to do it

Supervisor: *(Begin by asking your employee to share his self-analysis)* Let's begin by talking about how you think you're doing on your job. I'd like you to start by telling me several things you think you do particularly well. Please give me specific examples.

Employee: Okay...*(Very unsure)*

Supervisor: For instance, if I were asked to do a self-analysis, I'd mention my skill at prioritizing the work for my employees. To give an example, I would say, "I am very direct in outlining work assignments and when I expect things to be done." Do you understand what I mean and can you do this for me?

Employee: Yes. I relate well to the customer. *(Pause)* I think I'm flexible. *(Pause)* I also think I'm good at responding quickly in emergency situations. *(Pause looking serious and thoughtful)*

Supervisor: Good. I heard you mention three things. One, you're good at relating to the customers. Two, you're flexible. And three, you respond quickly in emergency situations. In what ways are you good at relating to customers? What are some of the things you do that lead you to conclude that this is a strong point?

Employee: Many customers are fearful when they come here. They are expecting to have a lot of trouble getting their problems resolved. I try to change the situation to a positive one by becoming someone they can relate to when they're here. I try to make sure they understand I'm listening to their troubles, and I give them assurance that something will be done.

Supervisor: *(Pausing to make sure the employee is finished)* I see. You're good at relating to customers because you reduce the fearfulness of the situation by becoming their ally, letting them know you care that their problem is solved. Is that right?

Employee: Right. I think things like that are really important.

Supervisor: Very important. *(Pause)* Let's move to another area. You said you thought you were very good at emergencies. How did you mean that?

Employee: Do you remember the Davis case? There was a lot of tension in that situation. I wasn't nervous or scared during the entire episode.

Supervisor: Okay. Now let's identify several areas where you need to improve your work performance, those areas where you aren't performing as effectively as you might be. I'd like you to think about some of the specific things you'd actually do to improve in each area. *(Pause)* For example, one of the areas where I'd like to improve is handling conflicts between our department and other departments. One thing I know I could do to improve is to have the departments sit down together, rather than meet with me one at a time. Do you understand?

Employee: Don't you think you're in a better position to tell me what areas I need to improve? You're familiar with my work, and you're my boss!

Supervisor: Yes, but for now I'd like to get some of your thoughts. I'll give you my suggestions later.

Employee: Okay. Let's see. The biggest thing, and I know you'll agree because you've reminded me of it, has to do with the customer service reports. I definitely think I can improve by writing up those reports when I finish each project. Another thing has to do with being better about getting here on time, especially when we're near the end of the month. *(Smiling)*

Supervisor: Yes...*(Pause)* So two areas where you could improve are being more conscientious about writing up customer service reports and getting to work on time. Anything else?

Employee: No, I can't think of anything right now.

Supervisor: Let's start with the first area, writing up customer service plans. What are some specific things you'd do to improve your performance in this area?

Employee: *(Pause)* Well, I put them off until the last minute and I usually end up scribbling my notes so they're hard for other people to read. *(Pause)* Because I'm rushing, I sometimes forget to record important information.

Supervisor: Okay, so to improve in this area you'd have to take the time to write notes that are legible and more complete?

Employee: Right. If they were legible, complete, and on time, I would definitely say I had improved in this area.

Supervisor: *(Smiling)* All right. A little later, we'll talk about what you might actually do to achieve that goal. But now let's turn to the second area, arriving on time. What do you need to do to improve in that area?

Employee: *(Smiling)* That's easy! Just get to work on time.

Supervisor: Okay. But could you be just a little more specific? For example, if you got to work on time every day for the next 10 days, would you say you had achieved your goal?

Employee: Oh, I see what you mean. *(Pause)* Uh...I guess now I arrive just a few minutes late about once a week. I guess I'd say that if I cut that down to being late only once a month I'd have achieved the goal.

In this scenario you see that a give-and-take, cooperative tone has been established, helping the employee look at both the positive and the negative aspects of performance.

Chapter 6

Understanding Motivation

3 theories of motivation

What is motivation? Is it what you do to get others to do something you want them to do? Is it something that happens inside an individual that gets her to do something?

One theory of motivation holds that humans direct their actions to satisfy their own needs. Once a need is satisfied, it no longer motivates. Abraham H. Maslow, an often-quoted author on the subject, categorizes needs as follows:

self-actualization
esteem
belonging
safety and security
physiological

Supervisors determine at what level of need an employee is operating, and then ensure that elements in the workplace exist to satisfy those needs. Long conversations are often the way to understand what is going on in the employee's head.

Another way of looking at employee motivation is Theory X versus Theory Y, a concept advanced by Douglas McGregor. Theory X assumes people hate work, are not ambitious, are not responsible, and prefer to be told what to do. Theory X managers believe people work only as long as they are watched, must be told specifically what to do and how to do it, and must be closely controlled until they do it. Theory Y managers, on the other hand, push authority down, assuming employees have a natural interest and willingness to work and do well at their jobs. These managers seek out ideas from their employees, looking for better ways of doing things.

Another noted behavior scientist, Frederick Herzberg, performed research on motivation, identifying satisfaction and dissatisfaction factors among workers. He found achievement to be the strongest employee motivator. Small achievements act as motivators, which cause people to achieve even more. According to Herzberg, the second strongest motivator is recognition. One effective way to increase productivity, for example, is to provide opportunities for achievement, giving the supervisor more opportunities to reward and recognize.

Unfortunately, most supervisors spend a lot of time convincing employees that the good work they produce is normal—that what they achieve is somehow expected and what they are paid to do! Recognition takes numerous forms beyond raises, bonuses, or promotions. A major form of recognition is the positive things managers say to their achieving employees! Good supervision is recognizing the runners in the race who haven't won but are running better than they did before. So what can you do?

- Get out from behind your desk so you can discover more occurrences of achievement. Catch your employees doing something good.
- Recognize achievement immediately, the minute you become aware of it.
- Acknowledge that lesser degrees of failure are achievements; recognize them.
- Find more ways to show appreciation.

When you hire someone, you rent her behavior. When you are supervising someone, you direct and modify this behavior (not the person) in order to achieve the company's goals. Your goal is to avoid self-destructive behavior on both your part and the employee's part.

Communication basics

The major reason for performance problems is lack of direction and lack of feedback—in other words, lack of effective communication. You are responsible for making sure your message is understood. You must learn to "say what you mean and mean what you say."

Our mind thinks at least six times faster than we can speak. Messages that are seen, heard, and understood by doing are the most likely to be retained.

Because the mind receives information so quickly, it often reacts even before the message is completed. Instead of viewing communication as information transmission (as many do), consider it more as idea transmission. That is, say or do something that will cause that idea to appear in your employee's head *and* ask the employee to speak back, restating the idea so you have conclusive proof it's in there! In this way you verify that she is involved. You have to think of a way to make the employee say it, for example, by asking questions. Therefore, you can improve communications with your employees by learning basic questioning skills.

An effective communicator learns to ask preparation questions. Before you ever talk to an employee, you must master the nine key preparation questions:

1. What background information exists?

2. What specific behaviors are at issue?

3. What are the consequences if things go unchanged?

4. What is the immediate objective?

5. What is my long-range goal?

6. What are the benefits of changed behavior?

7. How can this issue be described in the present tense?

8. How can I support this employee?

9. Am I in control and ready to discuss this situation?

It's also good to rehearse questions you can ask if an employee is shy, very quiet, or resistant to your appraisal of her. Too often managers and supervisors find themselves talking too much during the appraisal and getting little or no employee feedback. Here are some ideas that can be used to draw out the quiet employee:

1. Inform the employee: "This position is important to our company and we feel we must make the best possible decision."

2. Ask the employee, "Does that make sense to you? Do you agree? What do you think we should do?"

3. Continue, "The more information we have, the better decisions we can make for our company and for you. Do you agree?"

4. State to the employee, "I feel it is important to talk directly with your peers. Do you have any problems with that?" (Watch closely for the reaction.)

5. Ask the employee, "When I talk with your co-workers, what will they tell me about...?" (Start with easy questions.)

6. Add a final comment, "I don't like surprises! Is there anything you would like to explain now before I talk with your former supervisors?"

Chapter 7

The Performance Appraisal Face-to-Face

Building employee participation

The questions we just looked at provide a good way to get into the heart of the interview and discuss the employee's self-analysis. In this section we'll look more closely at the techniques necessary to do so. Begin by realizing that you have already completed the hard part; you've begun the process by committing to deal with the employee, and you've set the time and place. Your objective now is to begin the interview so that you *maximize the employee's participation*. Let's look more closely at being face-to-face.

Make sure you do not begin a performance appraisal until you are in control of the issues and your emotions. Decide before the meeting the minimum action you will consider acceptable, what alternative solutions are available, and when you expect performance to improve.

Set the stage by minimizing distractions and interruptions. Clear your desk and your mind of everything unrelated to the current situation. Hold the calls and close the door. Make sure you have read all the necessary paperwork and that it is at your disposal.

Make sure the temperature in the room is comfortable, water is available, and that the employee will be seated in a comfortable chair. Make the employee, not the appraisal form, the center of your focus. Make sure to allow enough time for the meeting so you don't have to end the discussion before it's completed.

You can make the person feel comfortable and welcome by beginning with a little casual conversation to get things started, but do not spend too much time on this. Sit face-to-face with no desk in between you if possible. This way, your body language will send the message that you're both on the same team, both trying to solve a common problem.

Structure the meeting by using a topical agenda, a brief order of events, so the employee knows what to expect. Begin by explaining why you are meeting and what is planned. Make sure the employee knows that every employee will participate in one of these meetings. It's part of your job and theirs. Also, make sure the employee understands that you will not be talking about money issues, that another meeting will be set up for that purpose. Instead, the focus is to talk about job performance and setting objectives for the future.

Explain that you are going to do the following:

- Find out how things are going in general.

- Ask the employee to explain how you can help make things better.

- Review the objectives of the job and the job description.

- Listen carefully to the employee's self-rating.

- Offer your own rating of the employee's strengths and weaknesses. Form a general impression of competence.
- Mutually agree on future goals for the employee.

Handling employee questions

Answer any questions the employee may have at any time during this explanation. Acknowledge the question and the feeling behind it. Let the employee know you understand. Respond directly to the concern. Get the employee's reaction. Make sure you've addressed the employee's concern before you move on.

Understand the types of questions employees have. Questions usually take the following shapes:

- *Hostile questions,* such as, "Why do I have to be first?" or "Boy, are we going to talk about things you need to do, because there sure are a lot of them." These types of questions usually indicate the person is feeling threatened or angry about having to talk to you. Reflect the person's feeling by asking for more information until the employee has had a chance to vent his hostility, then move on to the heart of the interview.

- *Neutral questions,* such as, "How long will this meeting take?" or "What do you mean by 'goals'?" These are clarifying questions. Your employee is unclear. Keep your responses simple. Answer as honestly and directly as you can and then move on.

- *Questions of concern,* such as, "Will anyone else know what we talk about in this meeting?" or "Will all this go in my personnel record?" Your response needs to show that you understand the employee's feeling. Again, answer as honestly and directly as you can before moving on.

How to do it

Supervisor: Come in and sit down. Please relax. The purpose of this meeting is to evaluate your performance and for us to work out together the best path for your future. Have you brought the forms I asked you to fill out for today's meeting?

Employee: Yes, I have.

Supervisor: Excellent. I've filled out the same forms. I want to compare what we've written on these forms so we can see where we agree and disagree. You placed a great deal of emphasis on product changes, much more than I would.

Employee: Really? I enjoy that part of my job.

Supervisor: I really need your talents used in other areas. In fact, I'd like to see your time commitment changed by the next time we meet. Tell me, why do you think you spend so much time on product changes?

Employee: I think it's because the people in Department B are always coming to me with bits and pieces of things they want me to do or want me to change. Maybe we need better communication.

Supervisor: That's a good thought. I'll talk to the supervisor of Department B. Maybe we can get something more productive worked out.

This scenario started with a comfortable opening and then set a direct path to discussing what was on the supervisor's mind. Some employees will need to spend more time on finding out how things are going, as we'll see below.

Finding out how things are going

It's important to explore what's on the mind of your employee, thereby opening the door to mutual understanding. This sends a signal to your employee that you care about what he has to say, which is good for morale. It also clears the air for discussions to follow by giving the employee a chance to talk about his problems and concerns. This can be an early warning system! You gain perspective. By listening early, you build a give-and-take rapport with the employee that will be useful later. Remember, you are asking your employee to talk about his favorite topic—himself.

How to do it

Supervisor: *(Leaning forward slightly)* How are things going for you here at ABC Company in general?

Employee: Well, I guess things are going pretty well for the most part. That's a little tough to answer all at once. I really don't know where to begin.

Supervisor: *(Nodding and smiling)* Yes, I understand. Take your time. I'm very interested in what you have to say.

Employee: Let's see. Things have been going pretty well. I like it here much more than my last job in Department B. I love my job. The atmosphere's a lot more relaxed and people seem to enjoy what they do.

Supervisor: *(Nodding)* Yes...

Employee: Well, I guess—oh! The bonuses! Thank goodness for the bonuses! *(Smiling broadly)*

Supervisor: *(Smiling back)* Sounds as if you're pretty happy about the bonuses.

Employee: Am I ever! My daughter is in college, and boy, do those bonuses help!

Supervisor: Good, I'm glad you feel that way. Now, I'd like to hear about anything you don't like or any problems you've been having on the job.

Employee: Problems? *(Looking down and hesitating)* Ah...well, for one thing, the work load gets fairly heavy sometimes, and I have a little trouble keeping up. All the managers act as if their work is the most important. They expect me to do everything "right now." And they get pretty upset if they don't get what they want right away.

Supervisor: I imagine that is difficult. *(Nodding)*

Employee: They have no knowledge of the work the other managers have already given me, and they don't seem to care about anything except their own work.

Supervisor: So you really feel major pressure at those times?

Employee: Sometimes I feel so tense I just want to run away. I don't know how to handle it. And then I start making mistakes. And that makes more work to correct, and I'm further behind!

Supervisor: I'm glad you told me about it. And I think there are a number of things we might do. *(Pause)* But let's talk about solutions to that problem a little later. I'd like to hear about any other problems you have before we get too deeply into solutions. I want to make sure I understand everything that is bothering you.

Employee: Okay. Well... *(Pause)* There is... *(Pause)* It's uh... *(Pause)* *(Much hesitation)* Susan... *(Pause)*

Supervisor: Susan?

Employee: I don't want to get anyone in trouble, but she can be very difficult at times.

Supervisor: When you say "difficult," how do you mean?

Employee: It's related to the work load problem. We're supposed to help each other when the crunch is on. I'll ask her for some help and she'll say that she's busy, but then she seems to find the time to gab for a half hour on the telephone while I'm breaking my neck to keep the managers off my back.

Supervisor: So you get pretty annoyed when she does that?

Employee: You bet! I guess I never realized how much I let it get to me. I've never said anything about it to her.

Supervisor: Okay, it sounds as if your main problems have to do with the work load, the pressure you feel from the managers, the mistakes that come from that situation, and Susan's unwillingness to help out when the crunch is on. Is that correct?

Employee: *(Nodding)* Right. And those really are big problems!

Supervisor: Yes, they are, and a little later we'll talk about some ways to deal with them. But now I'd like to move on to another subject. I'd like you to think about some ways I could make your job a little less frustrating and more satisfying for you. What ideas or suggestions do you have along those lines?

Employee: Let me see. Well, one thing is...I'd really like to know more about what everybody does around here.

Supervisor: So, you'd like to find out more about the nature of their jobs and how they fit into the big picture?

Employee: Yes.

Supervisor: What else can I do to make things less frustrating and more satisfying for you?

Employee: The computers in our department keep breaking down, and it always seems to be when we have deadlines.

Supervisor: Based on everything you've said so far, I need to work on three things to make life more satisfying and enjoyable for you around here. First, I need to speak to the managers about the work load problem. Maybe I can help them set up some kind of priority system so you don't get hit all at once with everything. Second, I may have to speak with Susan about being more cooperative when the crunch is on.

Employee: *(Nervously)* Are you sure that's a good idea? Will she know we talked? I don't want her thinking I'm a rat.

> **Supervisor:** I can appreciate that. But, believe me, I won't handle it that way. As I said when I asked you to meet with me, I'll be doing this sort of thing with everybody.
>
> **Employee:** Okay.
>
> **Supervisor:** Third, I think it would be a good idea if I arranged for you to meet some of the other people in the department so you could understand the roles they play.
>
> **Employee:** I'd like that.
>
> **Supervisor:** Great! And then fourth, I need to have the computers looked at. Okay, I'd like to move on to another topic: your work performance.

Before you begin your performance appraisal, recognize that discussing employee performance is where you are most likely to encounter initial resistance. Identifying problem behavior patterns helps set the stage for effective action.

One of the major types of problem behaviors is hostility. Hostile people bully or even overwhelm others; usually, they make critical remarks. Give the hostile employee time to run down. Don't answer shouting with shouting. Get him to sit down and keep eye contact. State your own opinions firmly and don't act frightened. Stand up to him without fighting. If the shouting continues, ask the employee to leave and come back when he has calmed down.

How to do it

> **Employee:** *(Agitated)* I tell you, some changes better get made at this company soon, or a lot of people are going to quit. And I'm not the only one who'll tell you that!

Supervisor: I hear a lot of anger in your voice. *(Leaning forward slightly)* I'd like to hear how you're feeling.

Employee: *(Slightly startled)* Well, I am really angry. I don't know whose fault it is, but we don't get much management. We're left on our own to make key decisions, and then we're criticized for making the wrong ones! Everyone around here thinks that the quality of management in this company leaves much to be desired!

Supervisor: *(Looking directly into the employee's eyes)* Sounds as if your anger has a lot to do with the direct supervision you're getting...or maybe that you're not getting. Isn't that anger really directed at me?

Employee: *(A little flustered)* I...didn't mean anything about you personally. Well...uh, that's not true either. It does have something to do with you.

Supervisor: I really want to hear what's on your mind, even if it is critical of me. Level with me and be as direct as you *can. (Puts down pen and faces employee, giving full attention).* What suggestions do you have for how I could improve the way I supervise?

Employee: Sometimes you give me a lot of work to do without telling me why I should do it. I waste a lot of my time doing things for no purpose at all. It makes me feel like I'm not important enough for you to take the time to make sure I understand. And usually there is no priority assigned to the work, so I'm never sure where I should start.

Supervisor: So one thing I could do is explain the purpose of the work I assign to you, giving a better idea of why I want it done, why it's important, and what priority it has?

> **Employee:** That would help a lot. A whole lot. And there are some other things if you're sure you'd like to hear them. *(Smiling)*
>
> **Supervisor:** *(Smiling)* I would like to hear them. Go ahead.

Often critical remarks are rooted in anger, resulting in hostility. In this scenario, you can see how the supervisor allowed the employee to vent his feelings and afterwards directed the conversation productively. Let's continue to learn from this exchange.

How to do it

Supervisor: You've been very honest with me, so I think I've got a pretty good idea about some of your problems. I'd like to wait to talk about solutions until a little later.

Employee: *(Interrupting)* What do you mean "wait to talk about solutions" until later? What's the sense of identifying problems if you don't want to talk about them? I just told you how upset I am and now you don't want to talk about how to solve the problems?

Supervisor: You're angry and irritated that I changed the subject before talking about solutions, is that right? *(Reflecting feeling)*

Employee: Yeah! I mean, it just doesn't make any sense. This whole thing is beginning to feel like a total waste of time.

Supervisor: You're saying that you want to talk about solutions right now, not after we've discussed anything else.

Employee: That's exactly what I'm saying, and I mean it!

Supervisor: I also think talking about solutions to the problems you mentioned is very important. I plan to spend a lot of time later in this interview to do just that, but I wanted to talk about some other things first. I'd like to hear your suggestions for how I could make your job more satisfying, and we need to do a thorough review of your work performance.

Employee: Well, I think it's more important to talk about solutions while the problems are still fresh in our minds.

Supervisor: Let's step back from this for just a minute to get a fresh perspective. It seems we disagree on how to proceed. You'd like to discuss solutions to some of the problems you identified right now. You feel it's important and you want to get it solved. I do, too, but I'd like to talk about solutions after we've covered some other areas so I have a good understanding of the total picture. I'd like to find a way out of this disagreement, preferably with a solution that we both can live with so we can get on with improving things for both of us. What do you think is our next step?

Employee: *(Pauses while thinking)* I don't really know. *(Smiling)* We can always do it my way. *(Laughing)* Well, we can maybe spend a few minutes talking about solutions to the things I told you were big problems to me. Then, if it looks as if we're not going to come up with any real solutions very quickly, or if we have more to talk about, we can talk about it again later in the interview.

Supervisor: Very good idea. Suppose we spend 15 minutes now talking about some potential solutions?

You can see how the emotion was controlled while a compromise evolved. The employee in this situation felt he was being heard and was playing an active role in the interview. This sort of feeling lays the groundwork for true communication.

Problem behavior and what to do in a performance appraisal

There are other types of behavior problems besides hostility.

Complainers are people who gripe incessantly, but never do anything about their problems. With these people you should:

1. Listen.
2. Acknowledge their feelings. Feelings are always valid.
3. Paraphrase the facts.
4. Move to problem-solving.

Unresponsive people respond only with yes/no answers or silence. Ask open-ended questions and wait patiently. Lean slightly toward the employee, using body language to show your interest, and inform the employee of what he must do to put the problem behind him.

Too agreeable people, while being very supportive, rarely produce what they say they will, or they act contrary to the way you have been led to expect. Bring to the surface the underlying facts and ask for their feedback, especially negative. Be prepared to move toward action, expectations, and deadlines.

Negative people always respond with comments such as, "It won't work." Your task is to present often optimistic but realistic statements about past successes while making sure the problem is thoroughly discussed both positively and negatively. Highly analytical people need sufficient time before you can expect them to act positively, avoiding negative tendencies.

Know-it-alls appear as condescending, pompous, imposing people who sometimes really are experts. Make sure you prepare yourself well before meeting with the "know-it-all." Structure your questions toward facts and then raise problems. Ask "what-if" questions to assist in re-examining your concerns.

Stallers slow down their decision-making until others make a decision for them. They have trouble letting go of anything until everything is perfect, which it never is. You must make it easy for stallers to tell you about conflicts or reservations that prevent their decisions. Listen for indirect clues that may provide insight into problem areas and give support after a decision is made. Try to keep any action steps as your responsibility.

Criers have problems controlling their emotions, and the tears show it. Often they are as embarrassed and as uncomfortable as you are. You can leave the room and let the employee gain composure, but identify the discomfort both of you are feeling as you leave.

Any of these behaviors can cause difficulty during a performance appraisal. When an employee refuses to go along with the game plan, you can use the *stop-look-listen approach*.

Stop-look-listen approach

- Stop the interaction before it becomes argumentative or unproductive.

- Don't get angry.

- Don't get defensive.

- Don't blame others.

- Don't lecture.

- Look squarely at the problem and describe it succinctly to the employee.

- Listen for suggestions and ways to resolve the problem together.

Another problem can arise when an employee talks too much. When this happens, decrease the use of verbal and nonverbal encouragement. That is, don't smile and nod as much. You can also cut down on direct eye contact.

Close the subject. Move to a new topic by setting time limits and reminding the employee of all that must be discussed. Reward concise answers with positive feedback.

Asking your employee how you can help

You may think you don't want to ask how you can help because:

- It's threatening.

- You expect the worst.

- You think the employee should ask the question, not you.

You *should* ask this question because:

- Employees love it.

- It gives you feedback on how you're doing as a boss.

- You'll begin to hear common themes.

- You'll gain perspective.

- It may unlock the door to increased performance.

- It lays the groundwork for creating performance agreement.

One of your objectives during the performance appraisal is to use your experience by adding to the alternatives your employee has to select from when faced with making a decision. Your employee may not see what you see, so help him.

Setting the course for action

Now comes the actual work of unifying all the elements into a constructive outcome by appraising performance and communicating the appraisal successfully to your employee.

The performance appraisal is a summary of your work observations. After each key area of accountability in your employee's job description is evaluated, his overall performance is evaluated. The results are summarized in the following chart.

Summary of Performance Appraisal	Future	Interview Objective
Satisfactory ⟋ Promotion		➜ Make development plans
⟍ No promotion		➜ Maintain performance
Unsatisfactory ⟋ Correctable		➜ Plan correction
⟍ Uncorrectable		➜ Fire or tolerate

Let's look at each of these areas by beginning with unsatisfactory performance. There are two types—correctable and uncorrectable. The most important question to ask yourself in contemplating how to correct unsatisfactory performance is "What is *influencing* poor performance?"

Consult your performance log. If you built your log correctly, after you observed a performance discrepancy, you should have *collected valid information* on your employee's performance and included it in the log from the onset. This eliminates surprises later. Your analysis of nonperformance should reveal trends. If there are no trends, you may have observed a simple blip that's minimally worth pursuing. But if there are trends, the formal, sit-down performance appraisal session is the place to address performance concerns.

You must be extremely careful when determining the reasons for nonperformance. What originally got your attention was a *symptom of nonperformance,* not the cause. You must make sure the employee knows precisely what he is to do so that his behavior can change. For you to effectively monitor and help the employee change, you must know precisely what the behavior or the problem is. Your performance log will help you with this. It will also help answer the question "Does the employee know that his performance is not what it should be?" Direct, specific questions should be asked on a day-to-day basis to clarify your log entries. Here are two questions you should learn to ask:

1. "Do you know what your error rate is?"
2. "Do you know how many days you arrived late for work in the last two weeks?"

Also look at your internal support systems. Feedback should not always have to pass through you to get to the employee. One of today's management goals is empowered workers!

This is a listing of common reasons why employees don't do what they're supposed to do. Use these potential reasons to organize yourself.

What's causing the problem?

_____ Not knowing what he is supposed to do.

_____ Not knowing how to do it.

_____ Not knowing why he should do it.

_____ Fear of future negative consequences.

_____ Experiencing personal problems.

_____ Not recognizing personal limits.

_____ Perceiving obstacles beyond his control.

_____ Thinking your way will not work.

_____ Thinking his way is better.

_____ Thinking something else is more important.

_____ Assuming no one could do it.

_____ Thinking he is already doing it.

_____ Being rewarded for not doing it.

_____ Receiving no negative consequence for performing poorly.

Remember, your employees must know exactly what you want in order to supply it, and they must know exactly what the consequences are if they don't. That's where your careful analysis of each employee's job description and your discussion of job duties, expectations, and consequences come into play. We will discuss preparation shortly.

Ask yourself if your objectives in this performance appraisal should be limited. Is there a limit to how much criticism your employee can absorb in one session? It may be too much to expect performance improvements in multiple areas within six months or even one year. However, you should know what improvements can be made and then gain the commitment from the employee to make them.

If you must select limited objectives, ask yourself the following questions:

- Which deficiencies are most critical to the company?
- Does the employee possess the confidence necessary to make the multiple changes?
- Can improvements be continuous, i.e., spread out over the calendar year, rather than tackled all at once?

Plan how you are going to help the employee accept the need to improve. Compliance does not necessarily mean acceptance, and the best results come from acceptance, from the employee stating that improvement is needed.

How much improvement is enough?

- Get the employee to commit to a specific plan for improvement.
- Distinguish between *improvement* and *correction*. Correction is the overall goal. Improvement is progress in the right direction.

If the performance remains unsatisfactory or is not correctable, or if the person lacks the capacity or the desire to improve, you have some options. You can continue to tolerate the unsatisfactory performance or begin a termination interview, no longer focusing on appraisal. Consult with the personnel department or your boss for information on how to proceed. Remember, once you decide an employee's nonperformance is occurring because of some unchangeable limitation, you have closed the door to other alternatives. You are no longer managing that employee, and you can only watch what happens.

Now, let's look at the employee who has satisfactory performance but has no chance of promotion. There are two types of people here: those who already know and accept the low probability of promotion and those who either don't know it or don't accept it. Every organization has people who should be promoted but won't be. These people are sometimes referred to as having "plateaued."

Those who don't accept their low probability of promotion will either rise, possibly in another company, or they will cause you problems.

Good performance does not, for many reasons, always ensure promotion. For the employee for whom there is no promotion ahead, you must define the employee's objectives clearly. Focus on these issues:

- What will sustain this employee's current performance? This type of employee will have a large need for positive reinforcement.

- What will motivate this employee? This question must be answered in terms of the person's immediate unmet needs.

- What specific motivators would be effective with this employee? Delegate often to him, transferring your authority where possible.

- How can you provide job enrichment, stretching his job to offer greater challenges? Different from delegation, such changes are permanent and can come from others' work as well as your own.

- Is it possible to encourage participation, giving a larger share in decision-making?

- Is this employee capable of being involved in mentoring other employees? Recognize that transferring knowledge is an important contribution to the success of the company.

Some employees don't realize there is no promotion ahead for them. They need to know their position clearly.

1. Hold the conversation in a favorable appraisal setting. Be supportive, explaining the outcome gently, and then look for ways to truly discuss the job at hand.
2. Try to identify possible blockages, while admitting that you don't have all the answers or control the promotion process.

By comparison, the interview for employees whose performance is satisfactory and for whom promotion lies ahead becomes a development interview, although promotion should not be guaranteed.

Your objective here is to shift the emphasis from present performance to preparation for a future job. Stress that development for the employee's next job does not overshadow the need to maintain satisfactory performance on his current job, but that the new duties will supplement it. Verify realistic employee career plans and together build the plan for the future.

Possible development actions include:

- On-the-job development.
- Personal coaching.
- Planned exposure to new positions or duties.

- In-house or off-the-job development.
- Workshops, seminars, conferences.
- Self-development and self-study.
- College courses and advanced degrees.

You can consult the following general performance guidelines when you talk to your employee, whether the employee is performing satisfactorily or not, is promotable or not:

- Use your log and appraisal form as a guide only.
- Start with the positive.
- Establish as much agreement as you can between your analysis and the employee's analysis.
- Be ready to shift from talking to listening.
- Get your employee's reaction to your analysis.
- Give direction after the employee reacts to your appraisal.
- Don't promise anything you can't deliver.

How to do it

Supervisor: *(Nodding and then pausing for several seconds before speaking)* Anything else you want to add?

Employee: I really think that pretty much covers all the areas I wanted to talk about today.

Supervisor: Good. You provided me with a very complete and thoughtful analysis of your job performance and how things are going for you. You really seemed to get into it!

Employee: *(Smiling and obviously pleased)* Yes, I did.

Supervisor: Now, as I mentioned a little earlier, I'd like to add a few things to what you've said.

Employee: This is the part I've been dreading.

Supervisor: You're a little concerned about what I have to say about your performance?

Employee: Yes...as well as this seems to be going, I guess I am a little apprehensive. It isn't always the easiest thing to have somebody give you honest and objective feedback on how you're doing on your job. You're afraid to hear some things. You know they are probably true, but it's hard to face them. Especially, when it comes from your boss.

Supervisor: *(Nodding and smiling but saying nothing)*

Employee: That's all I was thinking...I guess I'm ready to listen. *(Leaning forward slightly)*

Supervisor: *(Smiling) I* asked you to start with the areas where you think you're performing well. I'd like to do the same thing.

Employee: *(Smiling)* Good. I don't mind starting there!

Supervisor: One of the areas where you felt you were performing effectively was in making presentations. I'm in full agreement with that. Three of our most demanding managers have told me that you make excellent presentations, and they don't hand out compliments easily.

Employee: *(Smiling and looking a little embarrassed)* That's nice to know.

Supervisor: Yes, it is nice. Another thing, our training department has asked if they could use you as an instructor for new employee training.

Employee: *(A little surprised)* No, I didn't know that. I am really interested in being able to do that.

Supervisor: I'm glad. Let's talk about that in more detail later.

Employee: I'm looking forward to it!

Supervisor: Another area that you mentioned you were doing pretty well in is following up on leads the sales people give you. Again, I'm in full agreement.

Employee: *(Nodding)*

Supervisor: At least three of our customers have told me they would never have considered, much less chosen, our line if it hadn't been for your persistent following up. That's exactly what we want our inside sales people to do.

Employee: *(Smiling)* I hope they weren't saying I was bugging them too much.

Supervisor: Now I'd like to talk about some areas that you didn't mention where I think you're performing effectively.

Employee: *(Smiling and leaning forward)* Sure.

Supervisor: A lot of the things you do around here have a motivating, almost inspirational, effect on others. Ever since we've been working together. I've noticed you're always trying to help the people here.

Employee: *(Smiling and nodding)* Yes, well, I would want someone to do that for me. I just do what's right.

Supervisor: *(Smiling and nodding)* I think "helpful" is a good way to characterize what you do. Let's talk about another area where I think you're performing effectively on the job. In fact, it's an area in which I think you could stand to improve. *(Pause)* I'd like to explain my thinking and get your reactions. And finally, I'd like us to reach some agreement on what you could work on to improve your performance over the next couple of months. *(Pause)*

Employee: Okay.

Supervisor: And after that, I'd like us to agree on what I'm going to do to help you improve in these areas.

Employee: Sounds good.

Supervisor: One area where I think you could improve is in handling objections.

Employee: *(Wrinkling forehead)* Handling objections? I disagree. I think I'm good at handling objections. In fact, I even keep a notebook on objections so I can come up with better and better arguments. I practice, delivering responses to objections so I can deliver them with confidence.

Supervisor: When a prospect offers an objection, such as it's too expensive or it's not compatible without other equipment, it's awfully tempting to come back with an argument to overcome the objection.

Employee: *(Nodding)* Absolutely.

Supervisor: But often the best thing to do is to get more information, draw the guy out. You want to get him talking.

Employee: If I drew him out, I would know more about what's bothering him and what he really thinks is important, what he really wants.

Supervisor: It seems you're willing to consider that as a possible strategy for handling objections? I admire that about you. You are always looking for ways to improve. Why don't we move on to another area? A second area I'd like to see some improvement in is meeting deadlines.

Employee: *(Shaking his head and smiling)* I knew those reports were going to creep into this conversation. I hate those reports, and you know it. They're a big waste of time. I'd rather be selling.

Supervisor: Sounds as if you find the reports unpleasant, almost as though they are an obstacle to getting more important things done? *(Reflecting feeling)*

Employee: *(Sighing)* Yes, that's just how I feel. I wish we could automate the process so the data would just be there as we made our calls.

Supervisor: I'm not big on paperwork either. On the other hand, if those reports don't get in on time, it causes lots of problems. Until we computerize the department, we're just going to have to do those reports. *(Pause)* Maybe at this point it would be helpful if you reviewed for both of us the specific ways your reports can get done. Okay?

Finalizing performance improvement plans

At this point in the review, you will identify:

- Specific tasks the employee is going to work on within a defined time frame.
- Specific tasks you are going to work on during the same time frame to help the employee improve performance, removing frustrations and roadblocks.

The next step is to develop a written record designed to help both of you keep the agreement. It contains these items:

- Specific tasks the employee can work on to improve his performance.
- Specific tasks for you to work on that will assist and support your employee.

• Specific tasks that will make the employee's job
  less frustrating and more satisfying, while
  building for the future.

The list of specific tasks you compile needs to be prioritized. It should contain short- and long-term objectives. Develop a plan of action that can be broken down into meaningful and achievable steps.

Use the following strategy:

• Ask what the employee would like to work on.
• Make additional suggestions on what you would
  like the employee to work on.
• Reach agreement on exactly what the employee
  will do first.
• Ask what you can do to help.
• Make additional suggestions, if necessary, on
  things you can accomplish.
• Reach agreement on exactly what will be done by
  you and when it will be done.
• Write it down.

How to do it

Supervisor: Why don't you take a few minutes to talk about the specific things that you'd like to be working on over the next several weeks, given all the things that we've talked about so far?

Employee: Maybe I ought to put the worst first. Once I get that under control, the rest will be much easier. I'll make a commitment to get those monthly reports in on time every month for...

Supervisor: Say the next three months?

Employee: That sounds reasonable.

Supervisor: Great. What else? *(Beginning to make some notes)*

Employee: Well, I would like to work on learning new products.

Supervisor: *(Nodding and making more notes)* We've got getting your monthly reports in on time for the next three months and working on new products.

Employee: I still would like to do a better job of getting interviews with prospects. But I'll need some help in critiquing how I'm doing it now. Perhaps if we could spend some time role playing, I could get better at it.

Supervisor: *(Nodding)* Okay. Sounds good. Anything else?

Employee: I think that about covers it. I can't think of anything else.

Supervisor: *(Glancing at his notes)* You mentioned getting all your monthly reports in on time for the next three months, learning new products, and doing a better job of getting interviews. Does that pretty much cover it?

Employee: Yes.

Supervisor: Before we actually write down the tasks, I'd like to add a couple of ideas. Then we'll pare down the list to a manageable size.

The interview would proceed with the supervisor and employee listing all the areas needing work, setting reasonable dates for things to be done, and discussing all the ways the supervisor can help the employee achieve the objective.

Closing the performance appraisal interview

In closing the review, ask for your employee's reaction.

- If an employee seems angry, agitated, or upset, devote time to talking about those feelings.
- Help the employee come up with a solution to the problem.
- If you have different ideas on how to proceed, use the stop-look-listen approach outlined earlier.

Share your reaction to the performance interview with your employee. If you are pleased, share your positive feelings. If you are not pleased, be honest without being brutal. Don't put the blame for what happened entirely on the employee. Try to stress the positive. Describe the specific problems briefly and objectively. Ask for suggestions on how the problem can be solved or avoided in future meetings, trying to reach a win-win status.

Schedule the follow-up meeting, and end on a positive note. Walk the employee out in a friendly manner. Thank the employee and tell him you are looking forward to the follow-up meeting.

Chapter 8

Improving Performance Appraisal Interviewing Skills

Skill building

Appraising and interviewing is a science. You can acquire the skills that can help you relate constructively and communicate more successfully with every employee. Study the following prime areas. Each affects your ability to concentrate, and each causes the employee to believe you care.

You must be aware of your *attending behavior*. This refers to your general behavior while you are interacting with the employee. Let's look at the basic components of healthy behavior.

1. Make eye contact. Look the employee in the eye when talking *and* listening.

2. Use good body language. Aim your body at the listener and lean forward slightly. Use your facial muscles actively, but naturally. Don't be a stone face, and don't forget to smile occasionally!

3. Use gestures to support your facial message. Minimize distracting mannerisms, overused phrases, or clichés. Don't reuse the same example, and don't let distracting mannerisms get in your way so that the employee pays more attention to your mannerisms than your message. Practice your delivery in front of a mirror or videotape a mock interview. Study the videotape carefully in order to improve your communication ability.

4. Vary your speaking style to improve the chances that your message is heard and understood. When you are serious, make your points slowly and with emphasis. When you are enthusiastic, speed up and raise your pitch.

5. Become skilled at asking questions and gathering information. Invite your employee to talk. Be prepared to stop talking and start listening at any time. You are not on stage or carrying out a monologue here. This is not a lecture, but a guided conversation.

6. As you become involved in discussion, focus attention on a specific topic, but give the employee latitude to respond. Get rid of the feeling of interrogation.

7. Watch for clues. Continuing to talk when you know a person is not listening is a waste of time. If the employee exhibits any of the following behaviors, it means she is not listening:

- Holding out her hand as if to say, "Stop."

- Looking confused.

- Rolling her eyes toward the ceiling.

- Beginning to interrupt.

- Constantly looking away.

What's the best way to avoid sounding like an interrogator? When questioning employees, the general rule is that it is better to be descriptive than judgmental, to be supportive rather than authoritarian, and to set a tone of equality, not superiority.

By being descriptive, not judgmental, you show the employee that you are interested in solving a problem, not in finding a scapegoat, someone to blame.

- *Judgmental:* "How could you do such a stupid thing?"

- *Descriptive:* "Can you explain what caused the problem?"

By being supportive, not authoritarian, you help eliminate resentfulness and defensiveness. It is better to show respect for the employee's ability to problem-solve.

- *Authoritarian:* "This is what you do to solve this problem."

- *Supportive:* "What do you think we should do to solve this problem, and how can I help?"

If you put too much emphasis on your position and power, you may create a barrier between you and your employee. However, if you seek employee opinions and share information, a feeling of equality is created.

- *Superiority:* "I used to do your job, and this is the way it's done."
- *Equality:* "This is the way this has been done in the past, but I would like to hear how you think it could be done better."

Remember, you learn more from listening than from talking. The first highly effective listening technique is *reflecting* or summarizing. This technique captures the gist of what the other person says, putting it in your words. It helps prevent misunderstanding and stimulates your thinking.

Reflecting an employee's feelings is a simple, two-part process:

- You identify the feeling behind the other person's remark: confusion, anger, frustration, excitement, determination, etc.

- You reflect the feeling back to the employee, beginning your response with words such as, "You're feeling..." or "Sounds as if you're feeling..."

When you respond to, reflect, or summarize an employee's feelings in this way, you send an important message: "I'm as interested in your feelings as I am in your thoughts and ideas."

Another fundamental communication technique is to speak in specific terms. Here are six ways to build effective communication skills during your appraisals:

1. Focus on closing; speaking "fuzzily" is distracting and unproductive.

   - Fuzzy: "Work on your attitude."
   - Specific: "I need more work from you when my reports are due. Okay?" Ask for more work.

2. Focus on the facts. Avoid emotionally loaded expressions or criticisms that include insulting words, such as, "That was stupid."

3. Watch out for exaggeration, such as, "That was the most ridiculous thing anyone could have said." Be specific and accurate in your comments.

How not to do it

You have a bad temper. Stop throwing temper tantrums.

How to do it

You need to work on staying calm. Let's talk about some specific ways to do that.

---

4. Watch your pacing and timing. Pause after your main points, giving them a chance to sink in. Make sure the employee stays with you. Tell her what you're going to tell her, tell her, then tell her what you told her.

5. Strive for rapport. Reflecting feeling captures the emotions. Reflecting does not mean you agree with a statement. Using this technique, your task is only to mirror the employee's statement.

6. Summarize frequently. Summarizing focuses the main points. Here are some points to remember:

   - You do not make change happen by lecturing.
   - We have little ability to get people to do things they do not want to do.
   - The way people function is somehow part of them. They do not change easily.
   - Resistance is softened when people feel they can discuss their opinions and be heard.

During the appraisal session, **you should do only 10 percent of the talking**. You are the catalyst of change, getting employees to do most of the talking. Most supervisors tend to dominate conversations. How do you change this?

Learn to be quiet and understand the value of silence. Silence rarely offends. It is normally nonjudgmental if accompanied by the correct, open attending behavior. The raised eyebrow with the expectant look, uncrossed arms and legs, and posture in which you face the employee directly are all examples of nonjudgmental silence that encourage your employee to talk.

Know how to use questions effectively. You must become skilled in the use of the different types of questions. Be conscious of the kind of responses a question will generate before asking it. **It is *the form* of the question that determines the extent of the response.**

Restrictive or *closed-ended* questions prevent thought-provoking answers and discourage productive discussion. Examples are: How long? When did you...? Who wrote this?

Primarily, three types of questions work in getting employees to talk. Use these as alternatives to restrictive or closed-ended questions:

1. Open-ended questions.
2. Reflective questions.
3. Directive questions.

Open-ended questions. Open-ended questions get at attitudes, feelings, opinions, and other useful information about the person. Examples include: How do you feel about...? What could we do to...? Why has this...?

Open-ended questions can be successfully combined with the hypothetical problem. Examples include: Suppose you were...? How would you do it if you were...? What action would you take if...?

Open-ended questions can also be combined with commands. For example: Tell me more... Give me more detail... Keep talking...

How to do it

Employee: Our results would improve if we modified the method we use to manufacture that part.

Supervisor: You're convinced the results can be improved?

Reflective questions. Reflective questions can help you avoid arguments, because you are responding without accepting or rejecting what the employee said. It shows that you understand, that you were listening, and that you heard what the employee said. This also implies that you understand how she feels. Reflective questions encourage employees to expand on what they have said, leading to deeper levels of communication and understanding. If an employee has said something illogical or untrue, hearing it repeated helps her see the problems in it.

How to do it

It sounds like something is really bothering you. Is there anything else you'd like to say?

Directive questions. Directive questions obtain specific information. Such questions are usually used after the other types of questions have been tried and communication between you and your employee is strong.

How to do it

If you're convinced the results can be improved, exactly what would you do and when would you do it?

Combining different types of questions in your interview will stimulate the employee to participate. Pick the tools that are best for the job.

Once you get the employee talking, how do you respond to keep the conversation going? Use responses that focus and encourage, or the conversation will go off track or stop. Refrain from one-upmanship. Your objective is to stimulate the employee to suggest ideas. If you argue the merits of ideas as the employee says them, you waste idea-giving time. If you reject ideas as they are given, you may punish idea-giving behavior and discourage further discussion. If you reinforce good ideas when they come up before all ideas are out, it's easy for the employee to stop searching. A productive appraisal depends on the interaction of ideas. Some of the best ideas come from bad ideas, so stimulate the process and get *all* the ideas on the table.

How to do it

Supervisor: Please tell me any problems you've been having.

Employee: The new computers are down more than they're up. Is somebody going to do something about that? I can't get my work done on time.

Supervisor: Sounds as if you're pretty angry about that.

Employee: I am!

Interviewing attitudes

1. Avoid being defensive yourself—the person with tact gets things done without hostility.
2. Think positively about where you're trying to go rather than being negative about where you are now.
3. Think about growth, development, progress, and accomplishment.

4. Don't use words that point to negative behavior. You are not trying to excuse the past, you're planning for a better future.

5. Don't use *never, ever, always, every time, invariably, without exception,* etc. These terms trigger negative responses. Avoid profanity. Your language should be tactful but firm.

6. Control the interview. Your control is essential to a productive interview and to getting the employee's commitment to plan an improvement.

7. Focus the interview so you and the employee have to work on solutions. Discuss possible ways to improve, and decide how to begin.

8. Decide together what help the employee needs. Decide what you need to do to accomplish high-priority tasks. Be specific.
   - State the nature of the improvement sought.
   - State the quantity of the improvement sought.
   - Define dates when progress is to be checked.
   - Agree on who is going to do what.

Stay the course and communicate your message. Remember, the formal, sit-down performance appraisal interview is conversation that gets somewhere. It has objectives, an orderly track, and results in concrete agreements. It is conversational, but the employee does most of the talking.

Another frequently overlooked but highly effective skill you should perfect is body language. Body language sometimes communicates more about a person's real feelings than the person can. The more skilled you become at watching body language and picking up on these signals, the more effective you will become during performance appraising. In the important and sensitive business of performance appraisals, it isn't an option, it's a necessity.

Equality can be expressed in everything, from the initial handshake to the image left at the close of the interview. It is important not to stand or tower over your employee during the performance appraisal, starting from the time you ask your employee to meet with you.

The next most important thing to watch is eye contact. Avoiding eye contact can indicate disagreement, an unwillingness to continue to talk, or dishonesty. Confident people have more eye contact than those who are unsure or attempting to conceal, and the duration of their contact is longer. Confident people blink less, hence they also seem to be better listeners.

Gestures are almost as important as eye contact. One of the key gestures is crossing the arms across the chest as if to protect yourself against the individual, sometimes indicating you'd rather not move. Different from a comfortable position, this gesture usually involves gripping the arms or clenched fists.

Your response should be to draw out the feelings of subordinates who have crossed their arms and find out what their needs are. Reconsider what you are doing or saying to employees who have crossed their arms, because they are signaling strongly that they have withdrawn from the conversation. Getting agreement on anything, even on entirely unrelated topics, becomes more difficult after the arms are crossed and a person has become defensive. Failing to recognize the early signs of discontent or disagreement results in painful and unproductive communications.

Another key body language signal to watch out for is posture. Slouching can indicate indifference. Does the employee look interested? If not, find out why. A confident and open person will talk without covering her mouth and will stand and sit straight in an open posture.

In a study of negotiating techniques, it was found that the atmosphere for reaching settlements was enhanced when negotiators uncrossed their legs and moved toward each other.

Crossing of legs and leaning away are parts of a family of behaviors that communicate suspicion, uncertainty, rejection, or doubt. Other examples of such behaviors include physically moving the body away from the person, having the feet or entire body pointing to the exit, sending a sideways glance, taking a sideways position, and squirming in the chair.

Watch your employee's body language for important clues. Even more important, evaluate your own body language so that it:

1. Sends positive messages about your openness, understanding, and willingness to listen to the employee.

2. Does not send messages of superiority, defensiveness, or closed-mindedness.

Chapter 9

Follow-Up

Lack of follow-up is one of the most common supervisory failures. Informal follow-ups begin immediately after the appraisal interview. Follow up immediately and touch base frequently.

Ask your employee to follow up with you. Be sure he knows you meant what you said about working together by staying on top of what you agreed to work on together. Answer any questions immediately. These actions solidify the two-way relationship between you and your employee and make certain that the spotlight isn't totally on the employee.

Reinforce changed behavior immediately! It is better to praise positive behavior than to criticize negative behavior. Do this as behavior occurs; don't wait for the next formal meeting. Changing behavior is hard work. Periodic encouragement from you is necessary to prevent the employee from returning to the inappropriate behavior. The most critical aspect of follow-up is *timeliness*.

The structure of the follow-up interview is similar to that of the original performance appraisal interview. Analyze both your employee's and your own performance.

- Have the goals been accomplished?

- In what specific ways have the goals been exceeded or missed?

- Why weren't the goals accomplished?

- What needs to be done to get them accomplished?

Review progress, ask the employee's opinion, and give your own. Verify agreement on all main points before proceeding to the negative issues.

Decide where you want to go. For example, if major progress has been made, you can afford to schedule the next formal follow-up meeting farther into the future. If little progress has been made but a lot of effort has been expended, you can renegotiate the agreement, adjusting the "when" aspect. You may revise your goals, taking smaller steps. If, on the other hand, little progress has been made and little effort has been expended, this may signal that a termination is in order. Ask the employee for solutions. Ask the employee to think about the consequences of nonperformance, such as demotion, termination, etc.

Your next step is to close the interview. Get the employee's overall reaction to how things went. Give your own thoughts and feelings, as well. Schedule your next follow-up meeting to make sure you and your employee accomplish your goals! End the interview on a positive note.

Chapter 10

Forms, Practices, and Checklists

Performance appraisal checklist

Preparation

_____ I have reviewed mutually understood expectations with respect to job duties, projects, goals, standards, and any performance factors pertinent to this appraisal discussion.

_____ I have measured job performance against mutually understood expectations. I have done my best to avoid such pitfalls as:

• Allowing bias/prejudice to be a factor.

• Not consulting my performance log and relying on my memory alone.

• Overly focusing on some aspects of the job at the expense of others.

• Being overly influenced by my own experience.

• Using trait evaluation rather than performance measurement.

_____ I have reviewed the employee's background including:

- Skills.
- Work experience.
- Training.
- Past performance.
- Attendance records.

_____ I have identified the employee's performance strengths and determined areas in need of improvement. In so doing, I have:

- Accumulated specific documentation to communicate my position.
- Limited myself to those critical points that are the most important.
- Prepared a development plan in case the employee needs assistance in coming up with a suitable plan.
- Identified areas for concentration for the next appraisal period.
- Given the employee advance notice of when the discussion will be held so that he/she can prepare.
- Set aside an adequate block of uninterrupted time to permit a full and complete discussion.

Conducting the appraisal discussion

_____ I plan to begin the discussion by creating a sincere, open, and friendly atmosphere. This includes:

- Reviewing the purpose of the discussion.
- Making it clear that it is a joint discussion for the purpose of mutual problem-solving and goal-setting.
- Striving to put the employee at ease.

_____ In the body of the discussion, I intend to keep the focus on job performance and related factors. This includes:

- Discussing job requirements, employee strengths and accomplishments, and improvements needed; evaluating results of performance against objectives set during previous reviews and discussions.
- Being prepared to cite observations for each point I want to discuss.
- Encouraging the employee to appraise his/her own performance.
- Using open, reflective, and directive questions to promote thought.

_____ I will encourage the employee to outline his/her personal plans for self-development before suggesting ideas of my own. In the process, I will:

- Get the employee to set growth and improvement targets.
- Reach agreement on appropriate development plans, set a timetable, and explain the support I am prepared to give.

> • Be prepared to discuss work assignments, projects, and goals for the next appraisal period, asking the employee to prepare suggestions.

Closing the discussion

_____ I will be prepared to make notes during the discussion for the purpose of summarizing agreements and follow-up. In closing, I will:

• Summarize what has been discussed.

• Show enthusiasm for plans that have been made.

• Give the employee an opportunity to make additional suggestions.

• End on a positive, friendly, harmonious note.

Post-appraisal follow-up

_____ As soon as the discussion is over, I will record the plans made, points requiring follow-up, and the commitments I made. I will provide a copy for the employee. I will also evaluate:

• How I handled the discussion.

• What I did well.

• What I could have done better.

• What I learned about the employee and his/her job.

• What I learned about myself and my job.

Goals checklist

Place a number in the "yours" column indicating the importance of your performance appraisal system in achieving the goals listed. Then, have your employees do the same and compare their responses with yours.

Scale:

5: Always; 4: Usually; 3: Occasionally; 2: Seldom; 1: Never

Goals	Yours	Employees
1. Increase employees' understanding of job role and employer's expectations.	_____	_____
2. Improve employee morale.	_____	_____
3. Uphold professional standards.	_____	_____
4. Increase employees' self-awareness of job performance.	_____	_____
5. Maintain discipline.	_____	_____
6. Reward superior performance.	_____	_____
7. Produce competition among employees.	_____	_____
8. Reinforce boss-employee relationship.	_____	_____
9. Improve employee performance skills.	_____	_____
10. Weed out inferior employees.	_____	_____
11. Increase employees' self-confidence and self-esteem.	_____	_____
12. Inform supervisors/upper management of employees' performance.	_____	_____
13. Basis for awards and/or promotions.	_____	_____
14. Improve supervisor-employee relationship.	_____	_____
15. Basis for changing financial compensation.	_____	_____
Other:_____	_____	_____

Key Strategy: Both supervisor and employee must complete the checklist.

Performance evaluation checklist

1. Valid
   - Has a job analysis been conducted recently to determine the duties and responsibilities that must be carried out if the job is to be done successfully?
   - Are performance standards based on the results of the job analysis?
2. Consistent
   - Is the system implemented consistently (does a procedure exist)?
   - Is the same system used for all employees?
   - Do people who do the same work get evaluated against the same standards?
   - Are managers trained to use the system?
3. Useful
   - Is the system perceived to be helpful?
   - Is there support from top management?
   - Is the system easy to administer?

Key point

The use of any decision-making procedure (i.e., test for selection; applications; resumes; performance appraisal forms for use in promotion, demotion, transfer, discipline, termination, and salary actions) that has an adverse impact on any protected group is considered discriminatory, *unless* that decision-making procedure accurately measures the qualifications required for success in the job.

☐ We're okay ☐ Review ☐ Action needed
☐ Person responsible _____

Documentation checklist

Directions: Use this checklist to ensure that you have included all important components of relevant documentation.

Date _____   Employee _____

	Actions	Date(s)
☐	1. Copies of previous performance appraisal	_____
☐	2. Documented evidence of performance problem	_____
☐	3. Verbal warning	_____
☐	4. Written warning	_____
☐	5. Personal interview(s)	_____
☐	6. Remedial actions:	_____
	• Type _____	_____
	• Attempted _____	_____
	• Documented _____	_____
☐	7. Consequences interview	_____
☐	8. Check with personnel department	_____
☐	9. Check with next upper management level	_____
☐	10. Check with legal department or other legal resource	_____
☐	11. Termination notification	_____
☐	12. Termination interview	_____
☐	13. Explain rights	_____
☐	14. Exit interview	_____
☐	15. Debriefing with staff	_____

Contracting with employee's action plan

Employee name _____

_____   _____
Date   Job Title

_____   _____
Time   Meeting Place

Specific problem to be addressed:

Strategy:

Action steps (expectations):

Timetable:

Handling problem employees

Establish misconduct policy

Examples:

1. Theft over $10.	4. Obscene/abusive language.
2. Sexual harassment.	5. Asleep on the job.
3. Major insubordination.	6. Leaving job without permission.

1. Oral notice *Tell 'em*	2. Written notice *ell 'em what you told 'e*
3. Suspension (Final written notice)	4. Termination

- Discipline is at management's discretion based on employee's position, employment record, and mitigating circumstances.
- Similar instances of misconduct will be handled on an individual basis.

Tips for discipline
- Fairness.
- Open-mindedness.
- Timeliness.
- Consistency.
- Objectivity.
- Documentation.
- Communication.
- Progression.

☐ We're okay   ☐ Review   ☐ Action needed
☐ Person responsible _____

How to get the employee to talk

1. Inform the employee, "This position is important to our company, and we feel we must make the best possible decision."

2. Ask the employee, "Does that make sense to you? Do you agree? What do you think we should do?"

3. Continue with the employee, "The more information we have, the better decisions we can make for our company and for you. Do you agree?"

4. Say to the employee, "I feel it is important to talk directly with your peers. Do you have any problems with that?" (Watch closely for the reaction.)

5. Ask the employee, "When I talk with your co-workers, what will they tell me about...?"(Start with easy questions.)

6. State as a final comment, "I don't like surprises! Is there anything you would like to explain now before I talk with your former supervisors?"

Written warnings—a short course

Before documenting unacceptable performance or behavior, be sure you understand the entire situation. Be sure you can answer the following:

Who?	Who was involved? Who reported the incident? Who witnessed the incident? Who was affected?
What?	What specifically happened? What were the results of the action or inaction?
Where?	Where did the incident occur?
Why?	Why did this incident happen—what procedures or rules weren't followed? What is the employee's reason for the incident or behavior?
When?	When did the incident occur? When was it reported? When was the employee given the proper procedures or rules? When was the employee given any other notices of unacceptable performance?
How?	How did this incident happen? What did the employee do or fail to do? How did it affect others or the department? How could the incident have been avoided?

There are some simple rules regarding written warnings. After you have investigated the incident or behavior, use the following as a checklist in preparing your document.

- Prepare a neat and readable written warning.
- Address the warning to the employee, date and sign it.
- Always give the specific details—who, what, where, why, when, and how—of the incident or behavior.

- Avoid subjective statements; emphasize association policies and procedures.
- Offer solutions and state objectives.
- Document the consequences of continued unacceptable behavior, e.g., "Failure to...will result in further disciplinary action up to and including termination."

Conducting a firing interview

1. Do your homework.
2. If the situation seems to call for it, have a "friendly witness" present during the session.
3. Give clear, specific reasons for the termination. Put these in writing, signed by both parties.
4. Help the employee realize that once the consequences were explained, continuing the unsatisfactory behavior was the employee's matter.
5. Focus the termination on unacceptable behavior, not the person.
6. If it is applicable, advise the employee of the implications of removing files, equipment, or other organizational property, as well as revealing trade secrets to competitors.
7. Not all employees will take termination calmly, although the termination should come as no surprise. If the employee becomes upset, these steps will help:
   - Listen.
   - Share.
   - Continue.

- Above all, stay in control of your own emotions. There's no need for you to feel threatened by words—you still work there.
  - If you are physically threatened and there is no one with you, call in someone else immediately.

8. Know company policies.

9. Let employees know where they stand with you. Will you provide references?

10. Help employees realize that termination is painful for everyone. You and the organization would like everyone to succeed—and you wish them well.

11. A final word: Your anxiety about the termination session is both normal and healthy—it is a sign that you are a caring, feeling person, involved with a difficult task.

☐ We're okay ☐ Review ☐ Action needed
☐ Person responsible _____

Index